To my children, may you be the change
we wish to see in the world. —Na'ima

For Mahran and Zain, stay irreverent and brave.
Love you. —Nadine

First American edition published in 2023 by
Crocodile Books
An imprint of Interlink Publishing Group, Inc.
46 Crosby Street, Northampton, Massachusetts 01060
www.interlinkbooks.com

Library of Congress Cataloging-in-Publication Data available
ISBN 978-1-62371-723-0

Illustrated with watercolor
Printed and bound in China
9 8 7 6 5 4 3 2 1

A Child Like You

Words *by* Na'ima B. Robert
Pictures *by* Nadine Kaadan

Crocodile Books, USA

An imprint of Interlink Publishing Group, Inc.

www.interlinkbooks.com

Somewhere, out there,
in the wide, wide world,
a child like you is
watching.

She sees the plastic
that litters the beaches
and kills the fish in the sea.
Their homes are in danger.
Their numbers are dwindling.

She wonders how long they will last.

Somewhere, out there,
in the wide, wide world,
a child like you is
listening.

She hears the cries
of children like her,
whose parents are fighting for life.
They just want to be safe.
Surely that is their right.
Seeking sanctuary.

She can't get them out of her head.

Somewhere, out there,
in the wide, wide world,
a child like you is
searching.

She scans the pages
of book after book,
searching for someone like her.
Her story is not told.
Her culture is not honored.

She is proud of who she is.

Somewhere, out there,
in the wide, wide world,
a child like you is
feeling.

Feeling lost, feeling afraid.
Feeling confused, feeling angry
about the violence,
about the suffering,
about the greed.

About the uncertainty...

because the world can be
a scary place sometimes.

But somewhere, out there,
in the wide, wide world,
a child like you is
seeing.

Seeing new paths.
Seeing opportunities.
Seeing a new way forward.

And somewhere, out there,
in the wide, wide world,
a child like you is
hearing.

Hearing her inner voice.
Hearing words of encouragement.
Hearing the roar of the crowds.

And somewhere, out there,
in the wide, wide world,
a child like you is
feeling.

Feeling brave.
Feeling creative.
Feeling inventive and free...

because the world can be
a hopeful place sometimes.

And somewhere, out there,
in this wide, wide world,
children just like you
are speaking truth to power.

Standing up for themselves,
championing others.

Seeing the change...
    making the change.

Being the change.

ABOUT THE REAL CHILDREN IN THIS BOOK

Greta Thunberg

Greta was born in 2003. Her campaign for action against the dangers of global warming began as a one-girl protest outside the Swedish Parliament in 2018 with the slogan "School Strike for Climate." Very soon, her example was being followed by millions of schoolchildren across the world. Greta's message is that children, to whom the future belongs, must make their voices heard now to get the adult world to act. Determined to show by example as well as words, she crossed the Atlantic in a sailing boat in 2019 to address the United Nations Climate Action Summit in words now famous: "This is all wrong. I shouldn't be up here. I should be back in school on the other side of the ocean. Yet you all come to us young people for hope. How dare you?"

Greta has received many honors and awards from the adult world, but she isn't looking for patronage or praise—what she wants is positive action.

Yusra Mardini

Yusra was born in Syria and represented her country at the age of 15 in the FINA World Swimming Championships (2012). Three years later she and her sister fled from the civil war in Syria. On the sea crossing from Turkey to Greece, the engine of their overcrowded boat failed. In rough seas the boat threatened to capsize and Yusra, her sister, and two other refugees jumped into the sea to help stabilize the craft and push it forward. After three grueling hours the engine was restarted and they reached safety. In Germany, Yusra was able to train again and in 2016 she swam as a member of the Refugee Team at the Rio Olympics. Yusra was appointed as the youngest ever Goodwill Ambassador by the United Nations High Commissioner for Refugees in 2017 and combines her swimming career with work to help the world's 65 million refugees.

Marley Dias

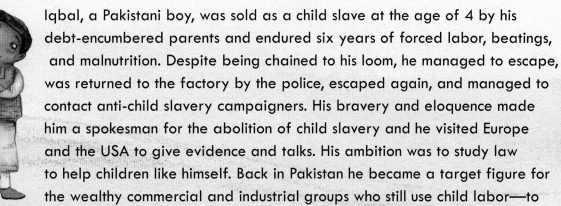

Marley was born in 2005 and lives in New Jersey, USA. Aged ten, she started her #1000BlackGirlBooks project when she realized how poorly represented black girls were in children's stories. She wanted to collect 1000 books in which black girls were leading characters, and send them to the school in Jamaica that her mother had attended. Marley also aimed to raise awareness of how much the school system was slanted away from black lives and culture. Her campaign won national and international attention and has resulted in a large increase in the number of books in which black children feature as leaders. Marley has written her own book about the campaign (which still goes on): *Marley Dias Gets It Done: And So Can You!*

Iqbal Masih

Iqbal, a Pakistani boy, was sold as a child slave at the age of 4 by his debt-encumbered parents and endured six years of forced labor, beatings, and malnutrition. Despite being chained to his loom, he managed to escape, was returned to the factory by the police, escaped again, and managed to contact anti-child slavery campaigners. His bravery and eloquence made him a spokesman for the abolition of child slavery and he visited Europe and the USA to give evidence and talks. His ambition was to study law to help children like himself. Back in Pakistan he became a target figure for the wealthy commercial and industrial groups who still use child labor—to maximize their own profits. Iqbal was tragically murdered in 1995 at the age of 13. No-one has been charged with his killing. Today there is an international Iqbal Masih Award for those who take action against "the worst effects of child labor."

From the Author

This book is a love letter to the next generation,
in whose hands the future of our planet lies.
Our world is complicated and it is important that we give
our children space and time to explore it, to ask questions,
to challenge assumptions, and dare to dream of a future
of their own making. For it is the hope and optimism
of children that continues to inspire adults like me to
write books that will, in some small way, shape the future
our children will go on to build.

From the Illustrator

When we started our collaboration on the development
of the book, I found it hard to choose only four
inspirational children from around the world to portray
in the story, as I knew there were many wonderful heroes
out there! But Greta, Yusra, Iqbal, and Marley have
inspired me on a personal level and I hope that
this book can inspire kids like my own children
to realize that you don't need to be an adult
to bring about real change for a better world.